Parents' Magazine Press   A Division of Parents' Magazine Enterprises, Inc.   New York

MacGregor Was a Dog

Story and pictures by Diane Redfield Massie

for Caitlin and David

M acGregor was a dog . . . .

who wanted to be an ostrich . . . .

more than anything else.

One day, while passing the dump . . . .

he found an ostrich suit.

It was bright pink.

He put it on . . .

. . . . and hurried home.

On the way, through the park,

two men drove by . . . .

in a yellow truck.

It stopped.

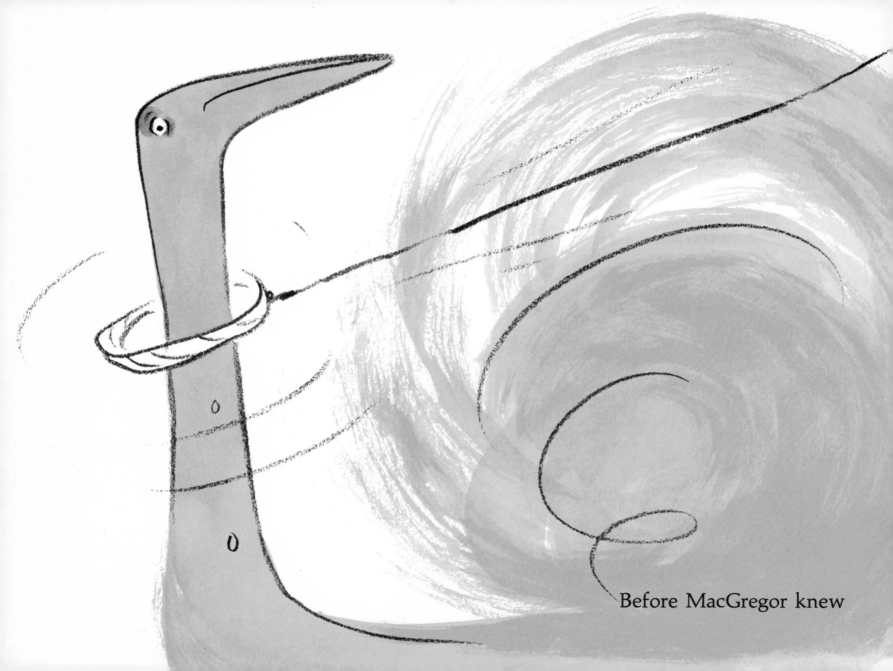

Before MacGregor knew

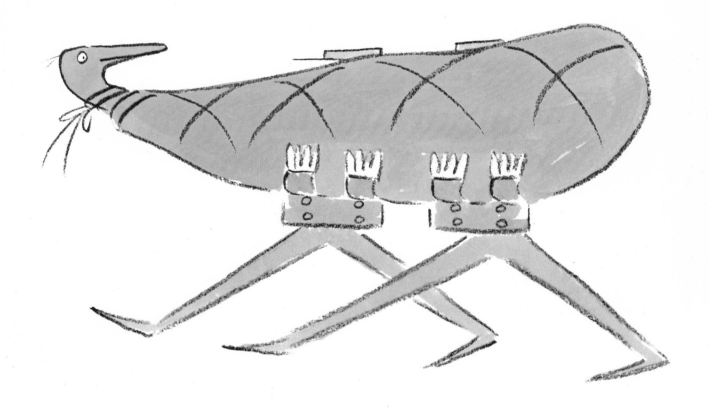

what was happening . . . .

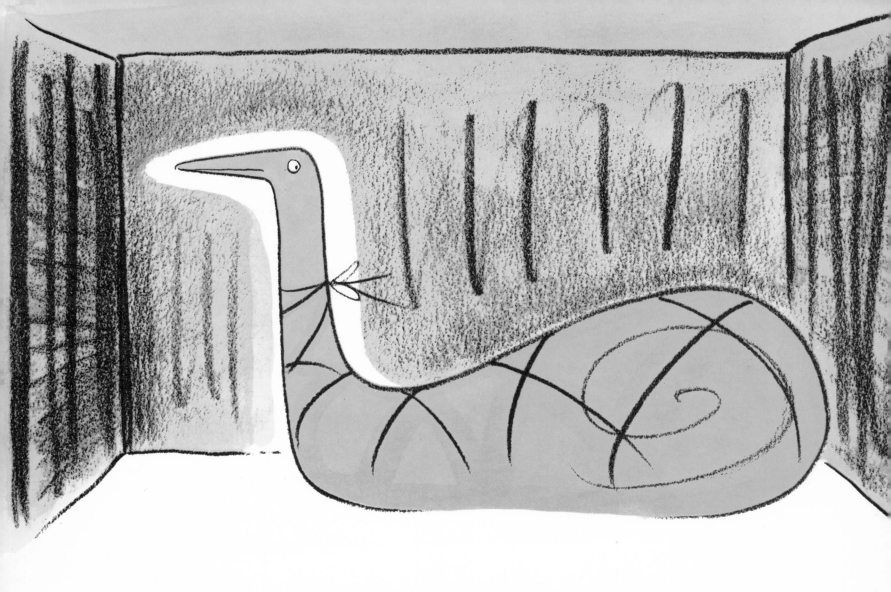

he found himself inside the truck.

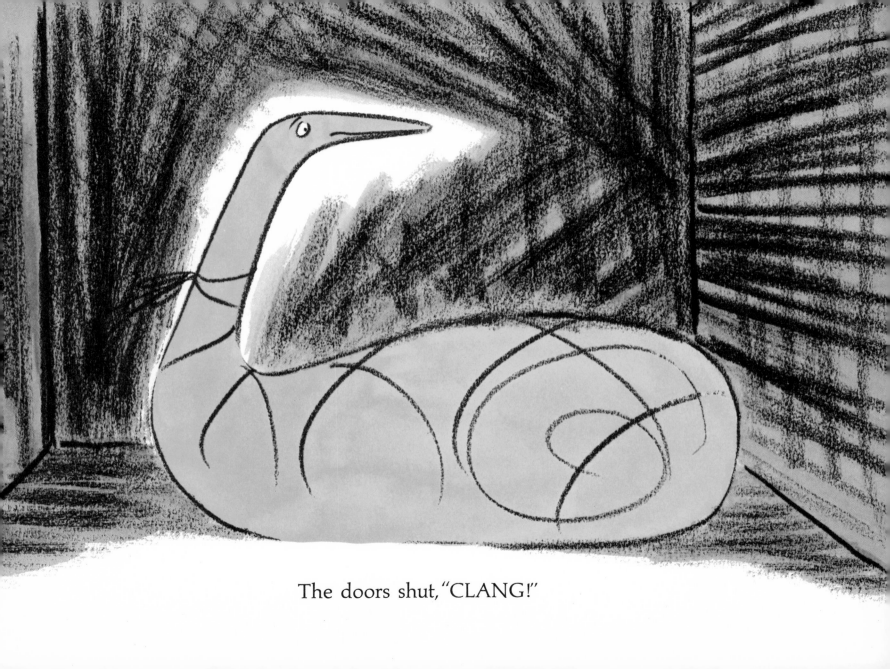

The doors shut, "CLANG!"

It was very dark.

Soon the truck stopped.

MacGregor was put into a cage . . .

with many other kinds of birds.

"They think I'm an ostrich!" said MacGregor.

"I'll bark so they'll know I'm not . . . .

. . . . and then they'll let me out."

The men came.

"It's even rarer than we thought," they said,

and they put MacGregor into a special cage by himself.

The next day, the paper said, "RARE OSTRICH AT THE ZOO."

The people came in crowds to see.

A little girl, in a yellow dress, came, too.

MacGregor barked when he saw her.

"THAT'S NOT AN OSTRICH," she said. "THAT'S MACGREGOR."

The attendants let him out.

They said they were very sorry . . . .

but MacGregor was so happy . . . .

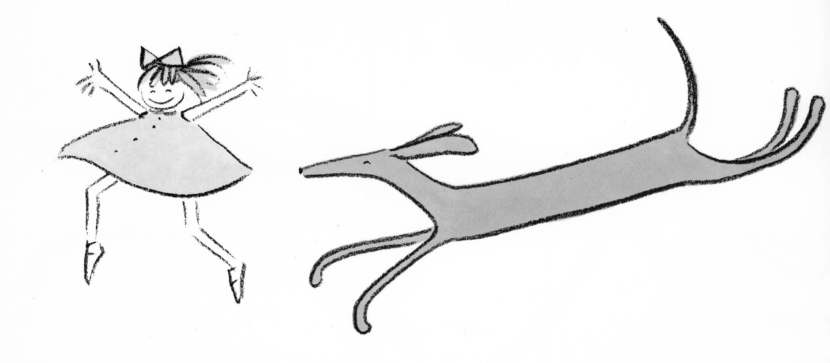

to be a dog again . . . .

that he wagged his tail . . . .

and hurried home.

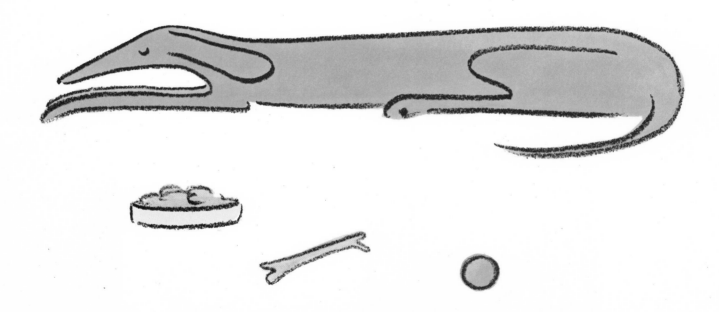